W9-BMW-690

DISCARD

Agassu
Legend of the Leopard King

Agassu
Legend of the Leopard King

retold and illustrated by Rick Dupré

Carolrhoda Books, Inc./Minneapolis

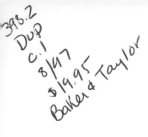
398.2
Dup
c.1
8/47
$19.95
Baker & Taylor

To my parents—I love you both

The artwork in this book was done in collage, which involves gluing objects onto a canvas. For these illustrations, the artist pasted images from African art and civil rights history onto his canvas. Then he painted the illustration of the story on top, using both acrylic and oil paints.

Copyright © 1993 by Rick Dupré

All rights reserved. International copyright secured. No part of this book may be reproduced, stored in a retrieval system, or transmitted in any form or by any means, electronic, mechanical, photocopying, recording, or otherwise, without the prior written permission of Carolrhoda Books, Inc., except for the inclusion of brief quotations in an acknowledged review.

Library of Congress Cataloging-in-Publication Data

Dupré, Rick.
Agassu : legend of the leopard king /
by Rick Dupré.
p.   cm.
Summary: Relates the traditional West African tale, based on actual events, of how the slave Agassu becomes free and returns to lead his people. Also includes brief biographies of nine African Americans involved in the struggle for equal rights.
ISBN 0-87614-764-3 (lib. bdg.)
[1. Folklore—Africa, West. 2. Slavery—
Folklore. 3. Human rights.] I. Title.
PZ8.1.D925Ag   1993
398.2—dc20
[E]   92-19691
                                      CIP
                                      AC

Manufactured in the United States of America
1 2 3   4   5 6 98 97 96 95 94 93

Introduction

There is something very special about an African folktale. Every time it is told, it can be a little different. It can change according to the teller's mood. It can change with the time of year. It can also change with the place in which it is told. These variations help make folktales lively and exciting.

Agassu's tale can be told in many ways, but one element is always the same: Agassu was a powerful person, and so were his ancestors.

This tale is told throughout western Africa, in the region now occupied by the countries of Ghana, Togo, and Benin. In this part of Africa, folktales are divided into two groups: *heho* and *hwenoho*. *Heho* are stories about people who never existed and events that never happened. *Hwenoho* are stories that are believed to be records of history. In other words, *hwenoho* are based on people who really lived and events that really happened. This story is *hwenoho*.

In Africa, as in the rest of the world, many people have been treated unfairly and have had to work hard to gain their rights. Agassu's tale is the story of one such struggle.

long the majestic coast of Africa, not so long ago, a pirogue glided across a wide lagoon. At the front of the fishing boat, the chief laptot called out the stroke to keep the other rowers in time.

The men in the pirogue were slaves. They were forced to work very hard rowing the heavy boat through the water.

Day and night, the slaves longed to escape the chains that bound them to the rowers' bench. Even though they were captives, they had not forgotten what it was like to be free.

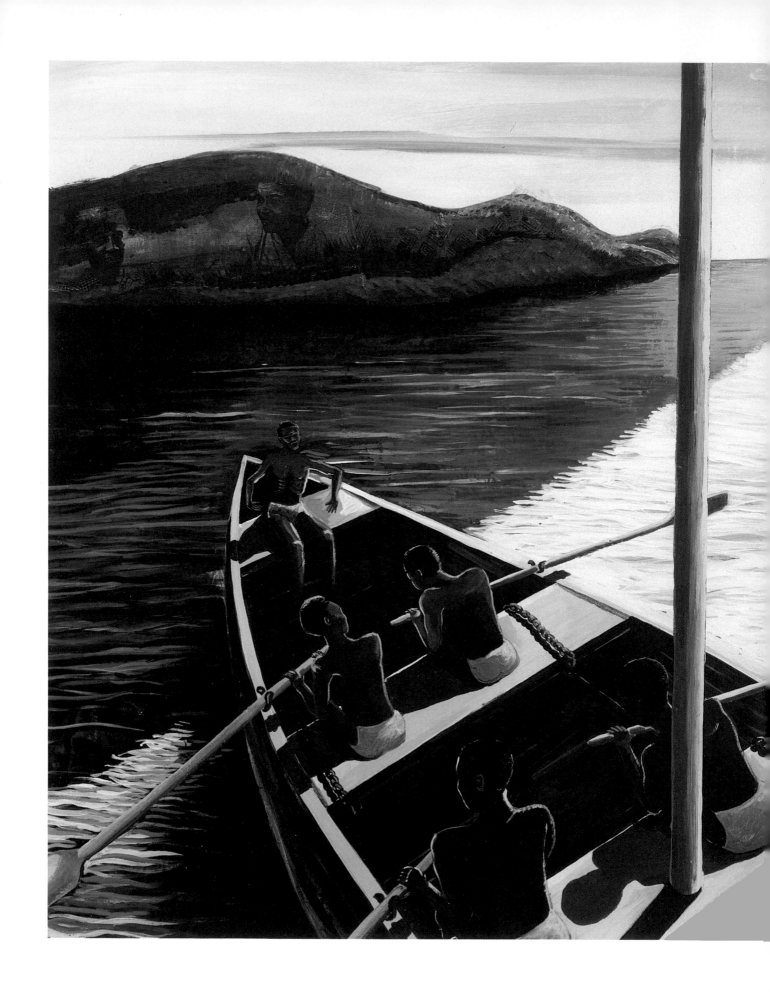

As the sun sank into
the sky and golden light filled
the sky, the slaves began to sing.
Their song was a call to the gods for
relief from sadness and pain:

> Call, brothers, call!
> Perhaps they will hear us.
> Our hearts are broken,
> the water has not yet spoken.
> Brothers, let us listen to nature
> and follow its lead…

And the boatmaster cracked his whip to quicken the
pace of the rowing.

One of the laptots was a young man named Agassu. He had been taken away from his family when he was just a boy and sold as a slave.

While Agassu was small and not yet strong enough to row, he was forced to work as a water dog. He could dive like an otter, so Agassu swam along the bottom of the lagoon and kept big fish from tearing the nets. Agassu loved the little bit of freedom he had when he was diving. But it was not long before he was strong enough to take his place on the rowers' bench.

The name Agassu means leopard. This was no surprise to the other laptots, for they could see the leopard's strength in him. His eyes were dark and deep and had a fierceness about them. His body was strong like the leopard, as well—strong enough to withstand the whippings of the boatmaster.

After a long day of rowing, the slaves would pull in to shore to rest. Sometimes they would be so near a village that they could almost feel the warm glow of family fires. They might even hear a hint of a girl's song. The peace of the land at dusk made them ache to join their villages once again.

In the villages, people were free, and they returned
from working in their fields and woods walking tall

and straight. Their proud bodies moved across the land like a field of corn blowing in the wind.

One starless night, a light breeze came up, and the boatmaster allowed the slaves to hoist the sail and rest. As Agassu drifted off to sleep, a voice spoke to him from far across the water. "I know you," it said. "Haven't you heard me calling you? I have something important to tell you."

Agassu thought he must be dreaming. But just then a wave came and bathed his forehead, and he realized the sea itself had spoken. Agassu's heart pounded in his chest. Why had the sea god chosen to speak to him? Agassu longed to hear the sea speak again. But the sea said nothing more that night and nothing for many nights to come.

Finally, after days of rowing, the wind came up again, and the crew was allowed to rest while the sail carried the pirogue. Agassu laid his head on the side of the boat and strained to hear the sea.

"Listen," whispered the sea. Agassu's eyes widened with excitement. "Listen while I tell you the story of a powerful family, my family.

"My story begins many years ago on the first day of spring. That day, all of the villagers came down to the shore to bring me gifts. Everyone sang happy songs. Strings, pipes, and drums sprinkled the air with music. The women adorned themselves with flowers and scattered petals in the surf. All the women were beautiful, but one woman above all the others captured my attention. When I looked into her deep brown velvet eyes, I could see only goodness sparkling there. I fell in love with her and asked her to be my wife."

That was how the sea spoke to Agassu on that second night.

19

E. P. CLARKE LIBRARY

Agassu was very anxious to hear more of the sea's wonderful history. However, only when the wind carried the pirogue did the sea continue its tale.

On calm nights when the slaves were forced to row, Agassu no longer thought about the pain in his body. Instead he thought about the sea's magical story. He was happier than he had been in a long time. He felt special because the sea had chosen to speak to him. And he knew that when the wind returned, so would the sea.

Indeed the wind did return, and the sail was hoisted. With the wind flapping lightly in the riggings, the sea's gentle voice returned. "Listen," called the sea. "I have much more to tell you. At the spring festival, I spoke with the beautiful woman and arranged to meet her at a rocky creek near the village. There, at Marriage Creek, as it is now called, she became my wife.

"We were very happy, and even happier when we had a son together. Our child was very beautiful, as are all children of gods. He was a little leopard cub, with black spots on a flame yellow coat. His eyes were intense and flashed like the deep sea.

"My jewel-eyed son married the daughter of King Tado of the Adja tribe. You, Agassu, are a descendant of this union. You are a descendant of the leopard and therefore a member of my family."

Agassu did not know what to say. He could not believe what he had heard. Imagine, Agassu-the-slave descended from the gods!

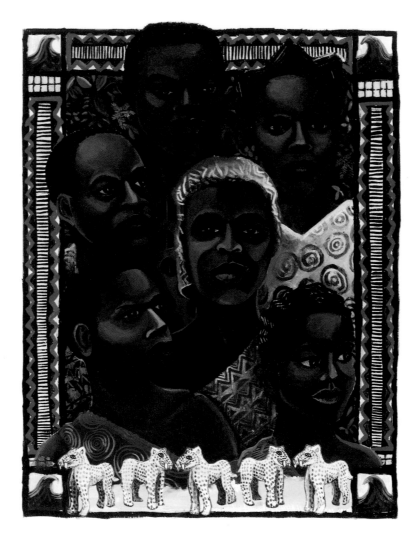

"Agassu, you are very important to your people,
for you are the last true descendant of the leopard,"
explained the sea. "You must have courage to meet
your fate, because soon you will be called upon to
fulfill an age-old prophecy. The prophecy says that
the sea will deliver the true son of the leopard to
his people, where he will take his rightful place as
king. You are that true son, Agassu, and your people
anxiously await your arrival!"

Agassu was confused. How could he return to his people when he was chained to the rowers' bench? Agassu did not have much time to think about it, for soon the quiet night gave way to another hot day of rowing. The boatmaster's whip whistled as he lashed the backs of his slaves. The laptots began to row through the water of another day, singing their song of grief:

> *Call, brothers, call!*
> *Perhaps the gods have heard us.*
> *Our hearts are weak.*
> *Surely one day the water will speak.*
> *It is the sea we must heed,*
> *Brothers, let us listen to nature*
>   *and follow its lead…*

The water *had* spoken to Agassu—just as the song predicted! He knew it was time to listen to the sea and break free of his chains. He could feel the leopard's strength in his body, and he knew he could remain a slave no longer.

Just then a storm came up. Winds whirled and the sea raged. "Have courage, Agassu," called the sea. "It is time for you to break your bonds!" Suddenly a bolt of lightning struck the pirogue with the power of all the firebolts in the heavens, and the chains holding Agassu and the other prisoners melted away.

The sea carried Agassu on the crest of a wave to the land of his ancestors. Its final message as it left Agassu on the beach was, "Remember what I have told you of your family. You possess the power of the gods, the strength of the leopard, and the goodness of your people. Use these gifts, and follow nature's lead. Now go forth and lead your people."

Upon the new shore, the darkness of the storm lifted like
a curtain, and the sun lit a world of green woods and beautiful
flowers. Agassu was dazzled by its beauty.

People—Agassu's people—began to emerge from the woods.

They had come to welcome home the true son of the leopard. As the prophecy had promised, the sea had delivered unto them their rightful king. The people rejoiced. They flocked around to welcome him and led him toward the village.

On the way, the elders of the village told Agassu how evil days had fallen upon their land. The people were forced to work very hard, yet they were still poor and hungry. The king and his two sons, however, were rich and well fed. They treated their subjects cruelly and punished anyone who complained or refused to work for them. The return of the leopard king was the people's only hope for happiness.

The villagers showed Agassu to a platform at the center of the village. "Take your place, Agassu!" they urged him. Agassu climbed onto the platform and stood between two ivory leopards. The people cheered. So much attention made Agassu a bit uncomfortable, but he understood how much his people needed a new king. Agassu was prepared to be that king, and he knew what his first duty would be: to face the evil rulers. The three men were brought before Agassu bound together like slaves.

The crowd shouted and jeered at the cruel men. Agassu motioned for silence. He then asked the three men if they had anything to say for themselves. The younger of the two princes raised his head and insulted Agassu. "You are an impostor!" he sneered. "The leopard king would surely bear the marks of his family on his body. All you have from the leopard is your name!"

The crowd was shocked at the prince's accusations. Agassu waited for silence, and then he said, "This man speaks the truth. I do not yet bear the marks of my family." Agassu then brought his hands across his face and chest. Sounds of drums filled the air and the crowd was mesmerized, for claw marks now crossed his smooth, dark skin. The prince stepped back, stunned and silent.

Agassu knew the people expected harsh punishment for the evil king and his sons. Some even wanted them killed.

Agassu thought of the sea's final command to remember his family. He heard the voices of his powerful father, the sea; his strong brother, the leopard; and his kind and good mother within him. Hers was the strongest voice of all, saying, "Be kind, for you too have known what it is to suffer." Agassu knew what had to be done.

"Hear me, my people!" commanded Agassu. "Release these men from their bonds as I have been released, and let no harm come to them." And to the three men who had brought misery to the land, Agassu said, "You are forgiven for the evil you committed. I do not know which way your steps will take you,

but listen, brothers. You too possess power, strength, and goodness within you. Use your gifts, and follow nature's lead. Now go forth from this place and find your own way."

These were the first words, this the first act, of the reign of Agassu of the Adja tribe.

The illustrations in this book tell the story of Agassu's struggle to be free. But look closely and you will see the faces of people involved in another struggle—the civil rights movement. These people faced hatred and inequality every day because they were African Americans. With the strength and fierceness they showed, they too could be descendents of the leopard. The lives of some of these great people are described below.

p. 37

W.E.B. Dubois was born William Edward Burghardt Dubois on February 23, 1868, in Great Barrington, Massachusetts. Dubois was an outstanding author, scholar, and civil rights leader who encouraged African Americans to educate themselves and to speak out against racism. In 1909 he helped found the National Association for the Advancement of Colored People (NAACP), an organization that uses legal action and social programs to fight discrimination.

p. 34

Ida B. Wells was born a slave on July 16, 1862, in Holly Springs, Mississippi, two months before the Emancipation Proclamation made slavery illegal. At the age of sixteen, Wells became a teacher, but all of her spare time was spent writing about and speaking out against racism. In 1891 she left teaching to become a journalist and activist. She devoted herself to exposing and ending the senseless lynching of African Americans in the South. Wells, like W.E.B. Dubois, helped found the NAACP.

p. 12

Frederick Douglass was born a slave in February 1817 in Talbot County, Maryland. In his twenties, Douglass managed to escape slavery and fled to New York. Once in the North, he became a leader in the antislavery movement. Douglass became an adviser to President Lincoln during the Civil War and held a variety of government posts in the following years.

Septima Clark was born on May 3, 1898, in Charleston, South Carolina. Clark trained to be a teacher and worked in the public school system until 1954, when she was fired for being a member of the NAACP. Clark went on to start the first citizenship school—a school devoted to training teachers to teach the skills that were needed to pass voter registration tests. (At that time, African Americans were required to pass a citizenship test before they were allowed to vote. The test was written unfairly to keep African Americans from passing.) Later, Clark set up similar programs throughout the South. Her untiring efforts gained her the title of "Queen Mother" of the civil rights movement.

p. 8

Rosa Parks was on born February 4, 1913, in Tuskegee, Alabama. In a life dedicated to the civil rights movement, Parks is most remembered for her December 1, 1955, challenge to segregation. She refused to give up her seat to a white passenger on a crowded Montgomery, Alabama, bus and was arrested. Parks's brave act led to the Montgomery bus boycott, which ultimately ended segregation on buses.

p. 8

Fannie Lou Hamer was born on October 6, 1917, in Montgomery County, Mississippi. Because her family was very poor, Fannie had to leave school after only six years to go to work. Hamer became heavily involved in the civil rights movement in 1961, when she enrolled in a citizenship school. She committed the rest of her life to the causes of voter registration and the war on poverty.

p. 37

p. 9

Malcolm X, born Malcolm Little on May 19, 1925, was the son of a Baptist preacher. As a child, he used and sold drugs. In 1946 he was sentenced to ten years in prison for burglary. During that time, he discovered the teachings of the Black Muslims and their black power movement. When he was paroled in 1952, he became an outspoken defender of the rights of African Americans. His willingness to use violence in the fight against racism created controversy among both blacks and whites. Malcolm X was assassinated in 1965.

p. 31

Robert Moses was born on January 23, 1935, in New York. At age twenty-five, Moses began his crusade for civil rights by volunteering for the Student Non-violent Coordinating Committee (SNCC). He dedicated his time with SNCC to black voter registration and managed to register over 60,000 people.

p. 18

Martin Luther King, Jr. was born in Atlanta, Georgia, on January 15, 1929. His inspiring speeches and belief in nonviolent protest made him a dominant force in the civil rights movement. King won the Nobel Peace Prize in 1964 at the age of thirty-five. His power and influence worried many supporters of racial inequality, and on April 4, 1968, he was assassinated. King's birthday is now celebrated as a national holiday.

398.2   Dupre, Rick.
Dup
               Agassu.

$19.95

DATE			

BAKER & TAYLOR